THE MISTLETOE BR

CW00797853

BY

J.P. REEDMAN

Author's Notes:

Christmas time is a traditional time to tell ghostly tales. While one might think legends of restless spirits would be reserved for Halloween, it seems that the fear of the 'dark season', the time when the days run short and illness is more likely to take hold, gave birth to its own set of haunting tales. *A Christmas Carol* is one of the classic modern Christmas ghost tales; others include the stories of M.R. James. Older, however, is the legend of the Mistletoe Bride, also known as The Mistletoe Bough or Bride and Seek. In this tale, a young bride on her wedding night plays a game of hide and seek with her groom, but accidentally traps herself in a wooden chest where she suffocates. Her bones are not found till centuries later, wrapped in the mouldering remains of her wedding gown with the dried-out shreds of a mistletoe wreath clinging to her skull...

I always found The Mistletoe Bride a particularly eerie and poignant story and looking it up, it occurs in various forms across England, being associated with several places—Bramshill House, Marwell Hall, Castle Horneck, Basildon Grotto, Exton Hall, Brockdish Hall, Bawdrip Rectory—and Minster Lovell.

As I have written several novels and novellas set at the time of Wars of the Roses, the later piqued my interest, since Minster Lovell was one of the properties of Francis Lovell, close friend to Richard III. I searched out the words to the old ballad associated with Minster Lovell and was delighted there was, in fact, a 'Lord Lovell' mentioned. And so I came up with an idea of Francis Lovell and Richard of Gloucester enjoying a festive Twelfth Night with their wives—till a strange storyteller wanders in from the cold and everything goes a bit wrong....(All events depicted such as the Lord of Misrule and the Mummers are based on traditional medieval pastimes; all poems in the text are my versions of the traditional plays and rhymes.)

Here are the first few verses of the original ballad about The Mistletoe Bride, written in 1830 by Thomas Haynes Bayly.

THE MISTLETOE BOUGH

The mistletoe hung in the castle hall,
The holly branch shone on the old oak wall;
And the baron's retainers were blithe and gay,
And keeping their Christmas holiday.
The baron beheld with a father's pride
His beautiful child, young Lovell's bride;
While she with her bright eyes seemed to be
The star of the goodly company.
Oh, the mistletoe bough.
Oh, the mistletoe bough.

"I'm weary of dancing now," she cried;
"Here, tarry a moment — I'll hide, I'll hide!
And, Lovell, be sure thou'rt first to trace
The clew to my secret lurking-place."
Away she ran — and her friends began
Each tower to search, and each nook to scan;
And young Lovell cried, "O, where dost thou hide?
I'm lonesome without thee, my own dear bride."
Oh, the mistletoe bough.
Oh, the mistletoe bough.

THE MISTLETOE BRIDE OF MINSTER LOVELL

The snow descended.

It fell, hissing faintly, over the winter-blighted lawns of the manor house, coating bare trees with their swinging branches and covering the ice on the edges of swift-flowing Windrush that form a tempting but deadly white lace that would crack beneath the touch of even the lightest foot. The cooks and servants kept their children well away—"Don't go there or old Green Jinny will have you!" they warned, waggling their fingers under inquisitive young noses. "She's there under the water, waiting for naughty children!"

In the doorway of the manor house, the Lord and his Lady glanced out into the snowy evening. Torches lit their way, the beautiful vaulted ceiling above them. Lanterns, rich men's toys, some imported from Italy hung on hooks too, bucking in the northerly wind and casting warm circles of light onto the snow.

"Do you think they will come even though the weather is foul, Francis?" asked the Lady, a small, slender girl with deep blue, almond-shaped eyes beneath feathery-light brows. She wore a gown of deep red brocade with silver traceries at neck and hem, and on her head was a truncated henin which revealed the slim crescent of her slicked back dark-blonde hair. "The night is foul."

"They will," said the Lord of the manor, Francis Lovell. "I am sure Richard is eager to get away from London and all those Woodvilles parading around like peacocks. Oh, he will arrive before long, I am sure of it. Him and Anne."

"I haven't seen Cousin Anne for ever such a long while. Ever since we came down here."

"I know, Nan…and yes, I know you prefer our house in Bedale or Mottram rather than this one in Oxfordshire. I enjoy both, but Minster Lovell is one of the great seats of my family, and I have plans for the manor house in the future…The old place needs tidying up. Perhaps a new tower or two, perhaps overlooking the river…" Francis grinned; he had a pleasant, attractive face framed by thick, waving sandy-brown hair. "What work is commissioned will, of course, depend on finances."

Nan Lovell had lost interest in talk of buildings and expenses. "Oh, Francis, I think I heard something…."

She took a step from the shelter of the porch into the whirling whiteness, laughing brightly as a haze of cold flakes dusted her nose and her veil. "The falling snow makes it so…so bright out, almost like day. A strange day. I almost feel a child again. I remember when it snowed at Ravensworth, my sisters and brothers would hold mock battles where we hurled snowballs at each other over a barricade of branches. Mother used to call us girls unladylike for engaging in such rough-and-tumble sport but we enjoyed it, and there was no one important to see…."

"You won't through a snowball at me, will you?" Francis had stepped out into the cold too now, his breath white around his mouth, the torchlight picking up fair highlights in his light-brown hair, making a nimbus of gold around his head. He coughed a little as the freezing air flooded over him and held his gloved hand to his mouth. It was always so in the cold season, an irritation of his lungs, a horrid affliction that he hated, but one that could not be helped by any doctor, no matter how skilled. His health had always been slightly precarious; he had been born a twin, coming into this world shortly before his sister Joan, and it was a great miracle both children had survived…and even thrived. But there were little complaints that bothered him…yet they were only small, trying but insignificant. He could ride, hunt and, most of the time, fight, and he held many manors and had good and loyal friends—chief amongst them the King's own younger brother, Richard Duke of Gloucester.

It was the young Duke who was coming here tonight, on this Eleventh day of Christmas—the Feast of Saint Simeon Stylites, who had spent thirty-seven years in prayer atop a stone pillar. That is, of course, if God willed it that Richard made the full journey from London through the snow, accompanied by his wife Anne Neville, Nan's cousin. Anne was, of course, the daughter of Richard Neville, Lord Warwick, who had fallen at Barnet Field, while Nan's mother was Warwick's sister, Alice. Both Richard and Francis had spent time in Warwick's household as youths, learning the knightly arts, and in both of them lingered a hint of sorrow about how things had transpired with Warwick in the end. First mentor…then turncoat.

But that was the past. The House of Lancaster had fallen and Edward IV sat triumphant and immoveable on the throne in his second reign. Anne, who had been hastily married to the Lancastrian Prince Edward on her father's wishes, had been widowed at the blood-bath of Tewkesbury, but after a not very happy period as a ward of George of Clarence and her sister Isabel, had married Richard. They had settled in the north, spending time between Middleham Castle and Barnard. Since Francis also had holdings in Yorkshire, he had consolidated his earlier fledgeling friendship with the Duke and saw him as family through their wives' kinship.

"I can see the shapes of riders on the bridge—they are coming!" Excited, Nan turned toward the church and the pathway beyond, her figure dark against the misty whiteness.

Francis blinked, the snowflakes sticking to his eyelashes and blurring his vision. "Nan, wait here…it will be more decorous! And you'll catch your death running out into such a storm!"

But in her eagerness, she was not listening. Up the path she flew, like a robin in her red gown, her cloak flaring behind her, past the snow-lashed block of St Kenelm's church, which Francis's grandsire William Lovell had rebuilt to replace a more ancient building dedicated to the unfortunate child-saint Kenelm, murdered by his sister in ancient times.

Pulling his cloak up over his nose against the biting cold of the winter's night, Francis followed his wife. The woods around the periphery of the hall's lands were dark, and although he had little fear that any outlaws or the like dwelt there, he could not bear the thought of Nan out alone…where she might slip or trip on the frozen ground.

As Nan reached the broad, trampled path leading to the village, the sound of the muffled clip-clop of horses' hoofs became fully audible in the dusky afternoon, along with the jingle of horse-bits and harness. On the far side of the neat little stone bridge that forded the Windrush, a party of riders appeared. Francis had ordered lanthorns placed upon the bridge parapets in anticipation of his guests' arrival; wan flames glinted amidst the swirling snowflakes, catching on the decorated bridles of the horses and on jewelled hatpins and cloak brooches of the riders.

The company proceeded steadily toward Minster Lovell Manor, riding against the wind. Nan glanced over her shoulder at Francis, puffing up behind her. She was smiling, happy as a child—'Listen!" she said. "Music. It is like hearing the music of…of angels!"

Francis paused. Sure enough, above the incessant whisper of the snow and the clack of the denuded branches twined above, he could hear music playing—shawm and hurdy-gurdy and lute.

"Richard has brought his players," he said. "He often travels with them. He appreciates music and only hires the most talented."

The riders had crossed the final arch of the bridge and began to wend their way toward the entrance to the manor grounds. As they approached, riding carefully down the slight incline toward the church and the grand house beyond, they looked almost like figures out of myth and legend, riders from the otherworld blown in upon the storm. Duke Richard and Duchess Anne rode at the fore, Richard on a tall grey, Anne upon a palfrey with bells knotted in her mane. Both were frosted by white, the snowflakes glittering on hair and brow; rushlights carried by their servants cast a golden aura over them.

Richard reined in his steed as he spied his friend on the path. "I did not foresee this!" he said. "Old Man Winter awaits me in the midst of the storm!"

"Old Man indeed—remember who is the elder, my lord!" Francis laughed. "Beware, Dickon—Nan was talking about her prowess in snowball fights earlier. I think I am also a good aim if pressed."

"Nan, look at your slippers—they will be soaked." Big-eyed, Anne Neville glanced down from her steed at her cousin with the snow rising about her toes. "And you'll freeze."

"You sound just like Francis. I am not so terrified by a bit of snow. Remember how it was in the north as young maids? You must, surely; Middleham must have been snowed in, even as Ravensworth was."

"Many of my Christmases were spent at Warwick instead," said Anne. "Father preferred it there during the coldest months. It, thankfully, was far less snowy there than in Yorkshire!"

The Duke of Gloucester's entourage continued on towards the door of Minster Lovell. The Duke dismounted and helped Anne down from her saddle, while Francis beckoned for his ostlers to take the tired, snow-streaked horses to the Minster's stables.

"So, this is the famous Minster." Richard glanced about, full of admiration. The two young nobles and their ladies stood in the lantern-lit doorway; overhead, the graceful arches of vault soared like the branches of slender birch trees, twined around great, heavy stone bosses carved into oak-leaves and roses.

"Indeed," said Francis, "the product of my grandfather William, who knocked down an older manor house to build something grander and more modern. I wish to add my own touch, but, as I told Nan—money is the problem."

Richard nodded sympathetically. "Is it not always so? Between you and me, Francis, my friend, recently the King decided to waive the taxes I owed him… several years in arrears . He said he was tired of asking, so he'd have my good service instead." He shrugged. "Do they not say money is the root of all evil? Well, it's true. I find it very evil to be short of money."

Francis snorted with mirth. "Come inside, Richard…before we all end up chilled to the bone and in the doctor's care."

Francis took his friend through the house, while their wives sought out the warmth and comfort of the solar and the household servants settled the Duke and Duchess of Gloucester's possessions into the spacious ground-floor apartments. The Duke looked approvingly at the Great Hall with its high, plastered walls and two eastern-facing windows filled with glass bearing the emblems of the Lovell family—a Silver Wolf, and a quartered shield showing the arms of Lovell, Deincourt, Holand, and Grey of Rotherfield, surmounted by an escutcheon with a crowned sable lion upon an argent background. Everywhere hung the decorations of the Christmas season—white-budded mistletoe boughs above the doors in huge green sprays, prickly holly dripping red berries on the mantle of the newly fireplaces, and coils of deep green ivy swirled snake-like around the multitude of iron and brass candelabras that lit the hall.

"The chapel is above, near the solar," said Francis, gesturing upwards. "My chaplain is at your disposal at any time. Your quarters for the duration of your stay are in the east range. The kitchen lies in the north with a bakehouse, buttery and pantry—I am sure you can smell the spices."

"I can," said Richard with mock mournfulness. "It had been a long, cold ride from London, especially with the inclement weather."

"You are hungry? I am not a very good host, am I?" laughed Frances. He gestured to a young squire with bobbed red hair. "Roland, get the Duke a goblet of wine. Bring some mince pastries while you are at it."

The wine was duly brought and the two friends toasted each other. A carafe of hippocras and a plate heaped with wafers and candied violets were sent up to the solar for Anne and Nan's pleasure.

"How was his Grace the King?" asked Francis as he sipped his wine. Francis was close to Richard, but despite the Duke's closeness to his royal brother, King Edward had never shown Francis much favour. Possibly a lingering punishment for his family's Lancastrian leanings—but others had decided to change loyalties to follow the White Rose without censure. Still, one must be grateful for the bountiful gifts one had already.

"Ned was very, very drunk last I saw him," said Richard, polishing off a mince pie. "As was Hastings. And Thomas Grey. The Queen was not pleased because Hastings had ushered some scantily-clad dancing women into the hall."

"Well, the King will never be as ascetic as Holy Harry Six, will he?" said Francis with a shrug. "Running from the high table at the sight of a woman's bosom!"

Richard spluttered on his wine. "How did you hear of that? It happened years ago! His prudishness was one reason why many believed Edward of Lancaster was not Henry's get."

Francis grinned. "It's legendary, Richard. Every young squire and scholar whispered of it behind his master's back. Did you not know?"

"I did not," said Richard, bemused.

"So…anyway, speak on—what did her Grace do when Hastings and her own dear son Thomas played the role of lechers at the Feast and tried to tempt the King from her side?"

"What could she do? There was only one thing for it, Francis. She called upon her brother Anthony Woodville to recite some of his poetry!"

Francis made a groaning noise. "Not the poetry again!"

"I am afraid so. It was too much even for Ned. He retired with Hastings and Grey in tow, so at least the rest of us could all depart the chamber. His departure left the Queen in an even fouler mood, however, although Anthony, as ever, took it in his stride. I suspect he may have even gone off to write another poem about the occasion."

It was Francis's turn to choke on a mouthful of wine. "Well, Richard, it will be quieter than that here at Minster Lovell. The maskers and mummers will be arriving late on the morrow, and there will be dances and storytelling."

"Storytelling?" Richard's brows rose.

"Yes, it's a tradition here for Twelfth Night. Old legends, old ghost tales are told."

"Ghosts!" said Richard mockingly.

"You believed in them once! Do you not remember that time at Middleham after Sunday Mass when you and I went up to the old castle mound, William's Hill, and ended up falling asleep under a faerie hawthorn, just like enchanted knights in a tale? When we woke, dusk had fallen and we both spied a man dressed in armour of an ancient date amidst the tangled bushes. When we called to him, he faded away…We ran screaming!"

"Mere fancy," said Richard. "We were idle, foolish boys who had, as I recall, stolen a ripe cheese from the kitchen and gobbled it down between us before falling asleep, sated after our crime. Cheese causes such dreams, I'm told. Served us both right. Warwick would have had us whipped if he'd found out."

Francis smiled at the memory of their youthful folly. "Be that as it may, the storyteller is coming with the mummers. If nothing else, his tales will bring terror to the ladies!"

Richard's brows rose again. "Really? Our wives are the granddaughters of old Salisbury and kin of the Kingmaker. I'd imagine if they decided to take on any evil spirit, or an over-zealous storyteller, they would surely prevail!"

The fifth of January, Epiphany Eve, dawned bright and sunny, the snow clouds sweeping away to reveal a sky of hard sapphire, unblemished by even a single cloud. The frosted ground glittered like a thousand diamonds, while icicles formed spears on bare tree-branches and along the roofline of Minster Lovell Hall. Every now and then, warmed slightly by the weak sunlight, one would fall with a tremendous crash, splintering against the packed earth below.

Francis took his guests, wrapped in their furred cloaks, gloved and hatted, into the gardens of the house. The grounds were bare now, the flowers all dead, the herb beds tucked beneath the blanketing snow. The garden was walled on three sides while the fourth side faced the river. Green-dark, the swollen waters of Windrush churned softly by, ice-sheets breaking on the surface under an onslaught of branches thrown into the river by the previous night's storm.

"In the summer there are roses in the garden," said Nan, "and lavender...but it looks very bleak now."

In the swinging bare boughs of the wind-whipped trees along the river's edge, a gaggle of crows were cawing noisily. The birds gazed down at the humans passing through the flowerless gardens, beady-eyed, hungry. Then, suddenly, the whole flock took off in a great black cloud, their wings blotting out the pallid sun for a brief moment.

"I am glad those scavengers are gone," said Nan, drawing her cloak tighter around her shoulders. "That cawing and croaking—like they were jeering at us."

Francis raised a hand to shield his eyes against the sun and followed the birds' flight off in the direction of Oxford. "Flying like that...I would wager there's another storm coming. Birds and beasts often know such things."

"But the sky is clear." Lady Anne turned her face up to the meagre warmth in the sky above.

"Perhaps not for long," Richard murmured. The clear, hard blueness of the early morn was passing. Little mounds of greyness began to bubble up on the horizon; the sky, although still blue, grew faded, filmy. A colder, more insistent wind began to blow, making the tree branches clack and clatter.

"North!" said the Duke of Gloucester, watching the way the dead curled leaves blew in the wind. "Whatever comes towards us, comes from the north."

"Quick then," said Francis, "before it grows too cold, I must show you some birds far finer than those ugly crows that spied on us earlier!"

The little party left the garden by a round-arched door and walked along the river bank. Frozen reeds stuck up; the dim water gurgled. The failing light shone off the surfaces of the nearby fishponds, frozen solid, pale mirrors.

Francis led his wife and friends around a retaining wall to a huge dovecot with a high conical roof. They were all glad to step through the little wooden door into the darkness beyond, out of the bitter wind.

"Welcome to the *columbier*," said Francis, gazing up.

All around doves nested in a series of holes grooved into the fabric of the dovecot. Their soft voices cooed in the darkness. "Oh," said Anne, reaching out to touch her face. "I felt something caress my cheek...like fingers."

"Feathers, my love." Richard of Gloucester caught a handful of pale fluff mid-air.

"The feathers are very soft," said Francis. "Best quality. All the mattresses and pillows in the house are stuffed full of them."

The doves continued to coo; outside, the wind was rising, rattling the red tiles on the conical roof. "I have some pairs that breed all through the winter," Francis continued. "The choicest squabs will be gracing our table tonight."

The wind howled again, a lonely sound almost like an animal's cry. "I am cold," said Anne, hugging herself. "Can we not go back now? The doves are very fine, Francis...but I would rather think of them as the lovely creatures they are rather than as food for the banquet."

Francis took up Anne's hand and kissed it briefly. "You have a kind heart, Lady," he said.

The four nobles left the dovecot. Outside the sky had dimmed appreciably; snow clouds hung overhead once more, a sullen, blackish wreath. The light had taken on the bluish colour common to cold winter afternoons. The trees were dancing in the gale and leaves skittering hither and thither, sailing down the iceless centre of the Windrush like a flotilla of elfin boats.

Suddenly a sound broke the cooling air—a noise like a pack of hounds in full cry. Only it did not come from the woodland but from the heavens. Louder and louder the sounds grew, an eerie belling and yammering.

"The Wild Hunt!" gasped Anne, her breath trembling in a white cloud before her lips as she gazed up at the heavens as if expecting to see a horned rider amidst the clouds, seeking to capture the souls of the damned while riding the storm with his red-eared, red-eyed hounds.

"It is only the wild geese passing over." Francis calmly gesturing to a break in the snow clouds where the wind had clawed them asunder. A V-shaped formation of birds was passing westward, their wings silhouetted starkly against the face of a revealed full moon.

"Nevertheless…as they fly onward, so should we," said Nan stoutly, crossing her arms. "It's too cold out here for man or beast—as you should know, Francis." She looked meaningfully at her husband; he flushed a little and suppressed a slight cough.

"Yes, yes, you are right," he then said, glancing toward the bulk of the house with its windows spilling light into the gathering dusk. "It is time I oversaw the preparations for tonight's feast. The rest of the guests will be arriving soon—unless the weather manages to prevents them."

The bad weather came to Minster Lovell, the snow howling in—but so did the invited, the cream of Oxfordshire's knights and nobles and many others besides, including members of the Stonor family, Francis' sisters Joan and Frideswide and their husbands, Lord Saye, John de la Pole, constable of Wallingford Castle (who was also Richard of Gloucester's brother-in-law), and the notorious Richard Harcourt, who had murdered his wife Edith and her supposed lover—then cheekily asked the pope for absolution so he could remarry. To everyone's surprise, he had been granted it and had wed Katherine de la Pole, who had brought a hefty jointure to sweeten the marriage.

The hall was full to brimming, the wine freely flowing, while Richard's musicians played Christmas songs with great cheer, as a troubadour in a fancy if old-fashioned chaperon stood on the far end of the dais and sang in a warbling, high-pitched voice,

"Tomorrow shall be my dancing day:
I would my true love so did chance
To see the legend of my play,
To call my true love to my dance.

"In a manger laid and wrapped I was,
So very poor, this was my chance,
Between an ox and a silly poor ass,
To call my true love to my dance."

Sing, oh! my love, oh! my love, my love, my love,
This have I done for my true love."

The troubadour's song was a not-terribly-respectful ditty about the Christ-child but most of the revellers were more interested in the dancing and the 'true love.' Men and maids spun out across the tiled floor, the candlelight catching on rich doublets with silvered buttons, frothy veils, paste gemstones and reams of seed-pearls.

At the high table, Francis and Nan sat with Richard and Anne below a canopy decorated with Francis' Wolf. Joan and her husband Brian Stapleton were at the next table and the recently married Frideswide with her new husband, Edward Norris. A great salt cellar stood near the dais; wrought from silver, it bore the shape of a mighty cockerel and moved about on wheels. Throughout the rest of the hall, the tables were laid with crimson damask cloth and fine bleached napkins; holly and mistletoe springs were wound around lines of trenchers and the stems of wine goblets. A gilt pheasant lay on a plinth and on either side of it an array of wondrous food—chickens boiled in egg-yolks and sprinkled with spices, hare pie and salted stag, sturgeon stewed in vinegar and decked with ginger, gilded plums and plums in rose-water, sugared cream with fennel seed topping. In honour of the Duke and Duchess of Gloucester, there was a massive subtlety fashioned into Richard's Boar badge from red-and-white jelly. The Boar's body was bright with silver foil and little red gemstones formed its eyes.

As the hour grew late, and the servers began busily tipping uneaten food, unfinished courses and discarded trenchers into the voiders, ready for distribution to the local poor in the morning, the steward of the house approached the high table and bowed. "My Lord Lovell, My Lady Anne, a troupe of mummers are without, asking admittance."

"Well, invite them in. We are expecting them." Francis leaned back in his seat. "Give them a drink and a mince pie—let no one say fine Christmas hospitality is not known at Minster Lovell."

The mummers entered the Hall, a rag-tag group in fantastical costumes that drew the immediate attention of the assembly, although nearly all of them had witnessed such performances before. It was an old tradition and a popular one.

First came a swaggering Saint George, wearing England's cross upon a white surcoat; behind him skulked a Saracen Knight, face ash-smeared and a turban on his head; a doctor in a dark, floor-length robe and cap, carrying a physics' bag of tools and potions—and at the rear, a sinister Hobby Horse that bucked and bounded around the Hall, nipping at hands and haunches and making all the assembled ladies shriek in feigned—or sometimes real—terror. The Hobby had an actual horse's skull with a clacking jaw that moved by means of strings; its body was a floating sea of white streamers rippling over a huge wooden frame.

The Saracen knight strutted up to the dais, pulling a wooden scimitar from his belt. Clearing his throat, he bellowed in a loud voice,

"Here comes I, a Turkish knight,
Come from Turkish lands to fight,
And if Saint George do meet me here
I'll try his courage—and stick him in the ear."

He made a fierce jabbing motion with his makeshift blade and the crowd first laughed then began to boo. The foreign knight, a heathen, was the antagonist of all mummers' play. Several candied plums flew past the actor's head, to go bouncing along the tiles, where they were chased by several hounds.

Saint George, a bell-shaped and short-legged man with a red moustache bristling beneath his helmet, marched purposely up to the Saracen Knight, drawing his own sword and brandishing it fiercely in the air.

"In comes I, Saint George,
that worthy champion, brave and bold.
Once with my sword and spear
I won three crowns of gold,
and fought the Dragon bold,
and brought him to the slaughter;
By that deed I won fair Sabra,
the King of Egypt's doe-eyed daughter."

Laughter erupted from the men in the audience, some ribald. "Was it your mighty spear that impressed the princess?" someone bawled.

The Saracen Knight seemed to take umbrage at the mention of the Egyptian princess. He took three long exaggerated strides towards Saint George, eyes flashing in the ashy mask of his face. He waved his fist under George's nose.

"Saint George, I pray you, be not too bold,
For if your blood is hot, I will soon make it grow cold!"

St George made a harrumphing noise and eyed his enemy with disdain. *"Thou Turkish Knight, now you must fear,*
I'll make you dread my sword and spear!"

With that pronouncement, Saint George and the Saracen flung themselves upon each other, battering away with their painted wooden swords, grimacing and yelling while the Hobby Horse, jaw clattering, capered in excited circles around them.

Saint George took one wild swing at his foe and clouted him on the pate. The Saracen Knight gave a theatrical groan and crumpled to the floor while the spectators on all sides of the Hall cheered wildly.

The mummer's play was not yet over, however. Saint George glanced around the chamber, peering into the sea of watching faces.

"Is there a doctor to be found,
Who can cure a deep and deadly wound?"

Out from the shadows shuffled the Doctor with his medicine bag.

"Oh yes, Saint George, now have no fear,
A Doctor of great renown stands here!"

Saint George looked the Doctor up and down, hands on his hips, dubious. "What can you cure?"

The doctor paraded around the fallen form of the Turkish knight, counting on his fingers.

"I can cure the itch,
the twitch, the palsy, the gout!
If the devil's in him, I'll drag him out!"

The doctor rummaged in his bag and pulled out a phial of blood-red liquid. Kneeling, he administered a potion to the fallen Saracen knight. He prodded him, poked him, and hissed the magic word "Abracadabra!" Then he leapt up, brandishing the empty phial, and roared,

"Once you were dead,
now you're alive,
the sap is in you—
I bid you—Arise!"

The Saracen Knight sprang to his feet with a flourish and then launched an onslaught on Saint George again. They tussled and tumbled until finally the Saint gave his opponent a great buffet with his sword that sent him tumbling back to the ground where he lay sprawled on the tiles. The Doctor looked down at him, shook his head and crossed himself.

Saint George prodded the buttocks of his slain adversary with his sword, eliciting mirth from around the Great Hall.

"Ashes to ashes, dust to dust,
into a hole, heathen Knight,
for there thou must!"

Uttering a wild neigh, the Hobby Horse capered up to the fallen Knight and threw its tattered robes over the limp figure of the actor, completely hiding him from view. There was much shuffling and bumping and the Saracen was carried from the Great Hall while the revellers clapped and cheered and raised their wine goblets.

Francis and Nan came down from the dais as the mummers re-entered and cordially invited them to join the feast at lowest tables, near the gaggle of excited squires and pages. Then, with a fanfare of horns from the gallery, the servers brought out the famous Twelfth Cake upon a wide silver platter polished until it shone like the moon. Leavened with yeast, the cake was heavy with candied fruits and scented by exotic spices—cinnamon and cloves. But it was not the cake itself that enthralled the crowd, who reached eagerly toward the servers to snatch a piece. It was what it contained. A solitary bean was baked into the fruit bread, and whoever found it would be crowned the Lord of Misrule at the feast and take his place at the high table. Anything could happen when the Lord of Misrule held sway—it was traditional for him to even command the great lords—just as, in many cathedrals on Epiphany Eve, the Boy Bishop ruled over the real Bishop for one single night.

"Jesu help us." Richard glanced up from his own slab of cake to watch his squires squabbling over the pieces of fruit in theirs. "I am afraid, Francis, that one of those rooting piglets of mine will swallow the damn bean whole without even realising it."

"As long as he doesn't choke." Francis eyed the squire's tables with some anxiety. "It would put an extreme damper on the festivities if one of the little bastards expired."

"Francis," laughed Nan, "what an awful thing to say."

"Well, we wouldn't have much to worry about. We have an esteemed Doctor present, after all." Richard nodded toward the seated mummer's troupe. The players still wore their costumes save for the Hobby Horse, who was now revealed as a bald, florid-faced man whose teeth were nearly as big and yellow as the horse's; the Hobby costume with its leering skull and tattered robes lay collapsed beside his bench.

Now it was Duchess Anne's turn to roll her eyes at her husband. "The two of you, Richard, Francis—still like the insolent boys who were the terror of my father's household..."

"We weren't, Lady Anne. I am wounded deeply!" Francis pressed his hand to his heart. "Wounded!"

"You were," she said, "I don't know which one was worse!" Suddenly her smile faded and an expression of sadness crossed her features. Many a Twelfth Night she had spent at Warwick or Middleham, competing with her sister Isabel for the accolade of being the best dressed or the best dancer, while their parents, the Earl and

Countess of Warwick, watched benignly from the dais. Now her father was dead, and her mother in retirement at Middleham, adjudged 'legally dead'. And Isabel lay dead in the crypt before the high altar at Tewkesbury. It had been around this time of year that she had died, no so very long ago, and her husband George had gone mad with grief and hung her maid and ranted of poison…. Dampness filled her eyes and she glanced away, a shadow upon her.

Richard laid his hand on her arm. "It was a good time, Anne. No one will ever deny that. God set us all on different paths, some that led astray, but we will not lose the memories." He glanced down, his own brow furrowed. He was thinking of George, his brother, executed by the King. Brother against brother.

The sombre moment vanished as a yell echoed through the Great Hall. For a moment, Francis wondered if his terrible prediction had come true—and one of the squires was indeed choking on the bean inserted into the Twelfth Cake.

But no. One of them, a gawky young lad of Francis' household named Filbert, was dancing around with his mouth agape, holding aloft a solitary bean as if it were a precious jewel. "I'm the Lord," he cried, "the Lord of Misrule!"

"And so you are," said Francis dryly. "And so you must have your crown." He beckoned to one of the servants who brought from a side-board a crown made of prickly holly twined with silver bells that chimed as it was lifted. Carefully he set it on Filbert's head.

Other servants then appeared carrying robes of green and yellow and a gold-painted chain of office, which they set about Filbert's shoulders. Scarves and ribbons and lace were wrapped around his neck, while around either leg twenty bells were tied on with coloured kerchiefs. The mummers joined in the crowning of the Lord of Misrule, the Hobby Horse prancing around Filbert, while the other hailed their new ruler, and pipers and drummers in the wings struck up a Devil's Dance.

"What does the Lord of Misrule command?" cried Francis, giving the still-dumbstruck Filbert a low, mocking bow. "Speak!"

"I…I…" Filbert stammered, "I command my fellow squires to dance on the table!" Whooping, the rest of youths leapt onto the nearest trestle tables, kicking their legs and twirling to the raucous sounds of bagpipes and tabor.

"I…I command everyone at Minster Lovell to drink until they fall down!"

"I will try my best," said Richard of Gloucester, beckoning a server to refresh his goblet of wine. All the men in the Hall followed suit. A few on the lower tables grabbed kegs from the servants and drank straight from them, spilling liquor across the floor.

"I want to ride the Hobby Horse!" The mummers surrounded the Lord of Misrule and lifted him bodily upon the Hobby's frame. The actor within the body of the grotesque horse began to buck and make neighing noises while Filbert clung to the neck, his holly-crown slipping, the bells on his legs all a-jangle, looking a right fool.

"Off on a wild ride you shall go, my Unruly Lord," cried the mummer dressed as Saint George, "or I will smite you with my sword!"

Whipping out his wooden blade, he struck the flat against the Hobby's flank. The Horse shot off around the chamber with the rest of the mummers' troupe speeding behind, beating its backside as they sang,

"I had a little hobby horse,
and it was dapple grey;
its head was made of pea-straw,
its tail was made of hay.
I sold it to an old woman
for a copper groat
and I'll not sing my song again
till you give me a new coat."

"I am not sure I *want* to hear that song again," said Richard with wry mirth, "but here, Francis—a groat for the mummers."

Francis stepped across the Hall to hand the coin to a very grateful Saint George.

Suddenly there was a clatter from the far end of the building, a skirl of icy wind, a shriek from the ladies seated nearest the commotion.

Into the Great Hall of Minster Lovell loped a strange, surreal figure. A man tall and spare, wearing a headdress surmounted by a stag's skull-cap with a spray of jagged antlers. Verdant and scarlet ribbons hung from every tine, along with holly, ivy and mistletoe. The newcomer's visage was painted green, giving it an unearthly appearance; his cloak, hanging low to the floor, was wrought of bleached wool, covered in snow from the storm which melted in the heat from the fireplaces to puddle on the ground around his battered leather boots.

Many of the knights in the room dropped their hands to where their swords would normally hang—but no one save the guards on the gate was armed other than the daggers they ate with.

"It's like the Green Knight from the tale of Gawain!" Anne whispered, leaning over towards Nan. "Who is he?"

Nan did not seem the slightest bit perturbed by the outlandish figure. "I presume it's the storyteller. We usually have one. I thought he would have arrived with the rest of the mummers but perhaps he became lost in the evil weather."

"A fierce creature he looks," said Anne. "Almost a devil."

The horned man had moved into the centre of the Hall. Everyone was silent, rapt; it seemed as if the fire sank low of its own volition, and shadows ran rampant around the Great Hall. Carved faces on the roof beams, jolly in the torch-glow, suddenly looked ugly, demonic. Outside, the wind could be heard shrieking over the high point of Minster Lovell's roof.

"Who are you?" asked Francis. "Give us your name, gleeman!"

"I have many names, good Lord, but Jack be the one I use most. Jack in the Green, old Jack Frost. Rhymer Jack when I tell my riddles and speak of old tales."

"Rhymer Jack it is, then. What tales can you tell us on this cold winter night?"

"A bitter night this be," said the storyteller, Rhymer Jack, "but not so bitter as the winters of long ago, when the wolves ran and the crows fed. In those years, the snow stayed four months and a shepherd who went out seeking a lost sheep often never came home again—his foul, reeking corpse wouldn't be found till spring…"

Some of the assembled ladies shuddered prettily; moved closer to their husbands, fanning their faces.

"It was in that bleak time when all the earth was dead as that lost shepherd, when the sun was swallowed by Satan himself, that a wedding was held here at Minster Lovell. A fine midwinter wedding to cheer the dark months…but which brought only heartbreak and tears…."

A murmur went through the Hall. Francis' sister Frideswide looked to her new husband. Comfortingly he took her hand beneath the table.

"The lady was the most beautiful woman in all of Oxfordshire— maybe all of England. Her name, though, is forgotten now—blown away like smoke…" Jack the Rhymer turned on his heel and approached one of the candelabras, blowing out one, two, three candles. Three thin blue smoke trails rose into the air; the room dimmed a little more. Shadows stretched long from the storyteller's antlered crown, reaching like fingers towards his now-silent audience.

"This peerless maid, her hair gold silk, her eyes blue as cornflowers, was set to marry the Lord Lovell. Right here, on this very spot." He stamped his booted heel on the floor, making a sharp noise that caused the dogs lounging by the fireplaces to leap up in fright and scurry under the trestle tables.

Francis smiled lopsidedly, a smile that did not reach his eyes; a tale featuring his own kin was not quite what he had expected. Haunting legends there were a-plenty that didn't involve the Lovell family—tales of Black Dogs and Barguests and night-walking Revenants. "I think you are mistaken, Jack," he said with mock cheerfulness. "This Hall was built by my grandfather, William Lovell. His wife Alice was my own grandmother, and not only were they not wed at Midwinter, I believe it was a rather uneventful affair and they did not suffer the matrimonial griefs you imply."

"Oh, my Lord Francis, it is not your grandfather William of whom I speak," said Jack. "Nor, indeed, of this particular house. My tale took place in the *old* house that underlies this one, the ancient house buried deep below, its green age-warped stones visible down in your cellars… Down there in the dark, the bones of the old house poke through the soil of its grave…."

Another series of mutters passed amongst the feasters as they looked at each other in confusion.

Francis tried to lighten the moment again, although he was increasingly perplexed and uncomfortable. "And how would you, Jack, know what lurks in my cellars? You haven't stolen in and started drinking my best wine, have you?"

A thin chorus of laughter went through the hall.

"I think we should *all* have more wine," said the Duke of Gloucester, also attempting to lighten the mood. "Then let this fellow finish his tale and send him on his way…"

The wine was duly brought, hauled up from the shadowy cellars Jack had mentioned. The storyteller paced the floor, caught in webs of shadows and candlelight, looking truly half-beast, half-man with his rack of great antlers swaying from side to side. "The marriage of that other Lord Lovell took place many hundred years ago, when the name Lovell was *le Lupe*…the Wolf…. One and all can still see the silver wolf of the family on my Lord Francis' badge and on the canopy over him."

Jack Rhymer gestured towards the dais and then, hunkering down on his heels, he flung back his head and released a bloodcurdling howl. The ladies all jumped. Irascible old Harcourt glowered. "What, in Jesu's name…"

Then the storyteller was up on his feet again, stalking about the floor in an almost agitated fashion. The mummers had now joined in his performance; one blew on a bone whistle, making an eerie high-pitched keening noise, as they circled round the gleeman, a procession of ragged figures in their outlandish costumes, the Hobby Horse bucking and dipping and nipping at their heels with its bleached teeth.

"The mistletoe was hanging in that ancient hall, just as it is tonight," said Jack Rhymer, gesturing to the large bundles of mistletoe, cut down from the nearby woodland and garlanded with red ribbons, that hung from the rafters and elsewhere. "Lots of pretty mistletoe with its white berries. Pretty mistletoe cut with a golden sickle, pretty mistletoe for handsome lordlings and their ladies to kiss under…."

He rubbed his hands; his teeth were white against the mask of his green-painted face. "Ah, a fine sight it was, dancing and gaiety and malmsey and a peacock in its feathers on the high table. The Yule log burned on the hearth; the Lord of Misrule danced a jig before the flames. But then that capricious Trickster suggested a new game for the wedding party to play—a game of All-Hide, of Hide and Go Seek, such as children play in the woods. Close your eyes, count to ten…then run to find your friends again…Only tonight there would be a twist, a change for the happy occasion—it would be a game of Bride and Seek."

The storyteller paused; above his head, one of the great two windows of Minster Lovell was filled by pale blue moonlight. The clouds had broken.

"The snow must have stopped," said Nan Lovell, glancing up. "The moon is out."

Jack Rhymer followed her gaze, reaching thin brown hands towards the wan, wavering light framed above. "The wedding was held on a night much like this one. Snow white as death, moon riding high like an old, worn skull. Just like the moon that hangs above Minster Lovell now."

"Cheerful," murmured Gloucester under his breath. Next to him Anne nibbled on a wafer, pretending nonchalance, but leaning forward slightly, clearly intrigued by the story even with its implied darkness.

The storyteller licked his lips. "The Lord Lovell was not pleased by the suggestion of this childish game. He wanted the wedding feast to swiftly end—and the bedding to commence…"

A ripple of laughter passed through the Hall. Goblets clanked. A bit of bawdiness always went down well in any such feast. "Sounds like a sensible fellow to me!" shouted one of the Stonors.

"Alas, the Lord's winsome little bride was entranced by the idea the Lord of Misrule suggested, and her maidens persuaded her a chase, a hunt would excite her husband's ardour even more. So, all the young people in the wedding party started to clamour to play Bride-and-Seek. Only the game would be played a little differently than usual. The bride alone would hide and the others would seek her. If a young man should find her, any young man, she must offer up a kiss to him—now *that* did not please Lord Lovell at all."

Jack Rhymer grinned; his teeth were long and brown, the canines sharp. Forget the Lovell's Wolf; he looked truly vulpine.

"Lord Lovell is not pleased now," Francis murmured under his breath. He had not expected such an unsavoury character as his Twelfth Night storyteller, making his guests uncomfortable with his posturing, howling and wild attire!

"Would *you* be pleased, Francis, if other men in the Hall wanted to kiss me?" Nan asked teasingly, nudging her husband.

"Of course I bloody well wouldn't...Nan, this is *ridiculous*. I am half of a mind to throw this uncouth oaf out into the snow."

"Oh, you couldn't. It would be considered most inhospitable! It is just a performance, like that of the mummers surely. And I...I want to hear what the ending of the story is. So does Cousin Anne. Even your sisters look intrigued." She nodded towards Joan and Frideswide, who, noticing the attention was on them, turned in Francis' direction.

Francis gritted his teeth, trying not to scowl. He did not want to argue with his wife—let alone his sisters, who had journeyed some distance to spend the Christmas season at Minster Lovell. "I will say nothing then, Nan, but he had better hurry up with his tale. You might find some enjoyment in it; I do not. And Richard looks most bemused." He gestured at his friend the Duke, who was leaning forward in his chair, fingers steepled, watching Jack Rhymer's performance with a bewildered frown.

The storyteller was pacing again, slow, sinuous; suddenly, he lifted off his antlered headdress and cast it clattering on the floor, making everyone in the Hall leap in alarm. Plates fell, cups clattered. The unmasking of the gleeman should have made him seem less otherworldly but as coils of grey hair fell writhing like ashen snakes spun around his bony shoulders and gaunt face, he seemed even more sinister, a gaunt lich escaped from some ancient tomb.

He was gleeful, darting about in the manner of a malevolent spider as he continued his tale: "So the beauteous bride ran through the great manor from chamber to chamber, while the merry host bayed behind her like hounds scenting blood. All wanted to *kiss* Lady Lovell."

Francis felt anger thread through his growing annoyance. He was by nature a calm man but he felt his fingers reach for his dagger's hilt. This troubadour, Jack or whoever he really was, was playing him, taunting him—he would not have it!

"Do go on!" said Nan, with Anne nodding furiously behind her. "We must know what happened next!"

Francis cast an exasperated glance at Nan and then at Richard who shook his head, almost imperceptibly and shrugged. He made a subtle gesture with his hand towards some of his personal guards who had made a silent appearance by the Hall door. If there was any trouble, the Duke was prepared to quell it.

Rhymer Jack was creeping close to the high table; Francis fancied he could see lice creeping through the man's hair so near was he. Repulsed, he was truly considering throwing him out now—but something restrained him. Was he under some kind of a spell? Or was it that really, underneath his disdain, he also wanted to know the ending of the tale? A shiver ran up his spine at the thought of witchery; this was the season of the Christ Child, but all men knew there were darker, older things abroad in the dark winter season too.

"But the lithesome young bride, with her fair gown and a mistletoe crown, was swift and quick, fleet as a deer," the storyteller went on, his eyes glittering in their deep sockets. "She fled from her husband, she fled from the young men with their bright eyes and hot hands. She fled from her maids, bored with their foolish chatter. She fled through the dark corridors of the huge house as the torches burnt to ashes…"

Suddenly, just as the gleeman mentioned the torches, there was a resounding bang. Someone, probably a servant in the kitchen, had opened an outside door, and a great gust of wind had blasted down the corridor and through the Great Hall, tipping over one of the less firmly-grounded candelabras. Candles rolled on the floor, smoking. The wreaths of festive mistletoe that had girded them sank into puddles of hot spilt wax.

Nervous laughter filled the Hall as servants rushed to collect up the expensive beeswax candles and right the candelabra. Rushlights and cressets were brought to bring renewed brightness to the dimming chamber.

"It's all right, my Lord Lovell, my Lady Anne, your Graces of Gloucester; it was just the wind!" said Francis' steward, embarrassed and flustered. "I will surely chastise the young muttonhead who left the kitchen door open!"

Jack Rhymer stood with his hoary head on one side as if listening for *something*—something none of the others could hear. "It is all coming to an end," he said, as if he guessed he was almost as the point of being driven into the night. "Do you wish to know the end, the bitter end of that night of celebration? Well, listen close, my lords, my ladies—listen close. The newly-wed Lady Lovell went up into the attic rooms at the top of the house, rooms full of forgotten things that lay like dead dreams covered in dust. And there she found the perfect place to hide—a heavy chest with great iron-bound lid. It was just the right size, almost as if it had been made to hold her…"

Anne and Nan both looked to each other, alarmed, perhaps guessing the ending of this unhappy tale.

"In she climbed," intoned Rhymer Jack, "and down fell the lid. She was in blackness, in darkness as complete as that of the grave…But she did not fear, not at first. Patiently, she waited for Lord Lovell to find her—for he would, wouldn't he? He would surely know every inch of his house. If nothing else, love would surely guide him to his bride…" His raspy voice dripped with ill-concealed sarcasm.

"I beg you say he found her and that all was made well," said Nan, her tone suddenly grown sharp. "I do not want to hear otherwise."

The man shook his tangled head in mock-mournfulness. "No one ever came to rescue her, my Lady. Down crashed the weighted lid; its hinges, red with blood-hued rust, jammed shut as surely as if a key had been thrust in the lock and turned. She was trapped inside and the chest was so thick that none heard her pound upon the lid, and no one heard her screams, for her copious bridal finery, her green wreath of mistletoe, muffled the sound…and soon, all too soon, the poor creature had no strength to cry out, for there was no air left for her to breathe in that makeshift coffin. And meanwhile, the merry game went on below with lords and ladies dashing to and fro, full of high sport, while the young Lord Lovell, missing his bride, became increasingly angry and afraid…

"They never found the girl, never…and Lord Lovell spoke of that fateful evening never again. Gossips said the bride had changed her mind and fled away, to a convent maybe. Or to the arms of another lover. But it was not true, oh no, never true—and on wintry nights Lord Lovell could hear a sound far away like scratching, like fingers clawing desperately to gain release from some prison, but to his dying day, he never could find the source…"

"Enough!" Francis leapt from his seat and approached Rhymer Jack with purpose. "Your pay, good man," he said brusquely, thrusting a small purse towards Jack." So now, farewell and good night to you. I dare say this has been an…*interesting* evening's entertainment, though not quite what I desired."

The man stared down at the purse with an unreadable expression. He did not take the money but instead gathered his ragged garb about him. "*Upon this night I seek no gain, but warmth of fire and pandemayne!*"

Whirling on his heel, he snatched a chunk of the finest white bread, the *pandemayne* or lord's bread, from a platter on the high table and then scuttled with spiderish motions for the Hall door. Some of the women in the hall shrieked in alarm and shied away from his rapid passage; men leapt from their benches, angry, ready to go after him.

"No, no, let him go," said Francis, bemused but secretly relieved the gleeman was gone. "He's clearly mad. Let him go out into the snow and gnaw his pilfered bread beneath some tree in the woods."

The Lord of Minster Lovell walked toward the rest of the mummers, who had clustered around the lower tables, seeking scraps, seemingly trying to disassociate themselves from the disturbing storyteller. "And you—are you not going after your companion?"

The actor dressed as Saint George stared at Francis in shock and dismay. "Milord, I beg yer pardon, but *that* one was never a member of our company! Never seen the knave before in me life. Crazy fool, moon-mad." He tapped his forehead.

"He wasn't with you?"

"We thought *you'd* hired him. To do the stories like, while we acted the play. Sometimes we perform with other groups from other places—tumblers and acrobats from Oxford, singers from Abingdon…"

Francis looked aghast. "So some stranger wandered into my home! He could have had any kind of evil intention."

"He was clearly mad, exactly as the mummer said," murmured Nan, coming up behind her husband and touching his sleeve. "We need not worry—he's gone now."

"He could be creeping about in the woods outside, waiting…"

"The door is shut against him. Tell the guards to admit no one without your say-so! You can send out searchers tomorrow…Let's not let this stranger's uncanny presence and silly legend ruin our Twelfth Night revels."

Francis let his gaze travel to the Duke of Gloucester. He did not want to disappoint his friend whose presence in his house he had so looked forward to. Nor did he wish to disappoint his family.

"No, I shall not speak of it again, I promise—not till the morrow when I'll make certain the vagrant is run off our lands," he said quietly to Nan, clasping her hand. She flashed him a smile that made his heart leap with pleasure. "Now, let us return to dancing and much merriment! Let us forget that strange wight blown in on the winter storm!"

He gestured to the musicians perched high in the wooden gallery overlooking the hall and they grasped their instruments and began to play the music for a *farandole*. He then guided Nan out into the centre of the hall while others swarmed to form the lines on either side Only the Duke and Duchess of Gloucester remained seated under their canopy, watching.

When the dance was over, the feasters had indeed become merry again, laughing and jesting about the odd stranger who had crept in from the cold to regale them with his rather unsavoury, gloomy tale. Filbert, as Lord of Misrule, was cavorting with the Mummers once again, quite drunk. Someone had painted his face like a blowzy woman's, with great rouged cheeks and a cherry mouth, and one of the mummers had come up with a Fool's Cap to replace his wilting and battered crown of greenery. The Hobby Horse was still snapping away at him with its sinister jaws, while the younger squires and pages were taking turns to thump him with a pig's bladder they had pilfered from the Saracen Knight, giggling all the while till tears rolled down their faces.

Suddenly Filbert sprang up onto the nearest table and wind-milled his arms as if he would fly off to the rafters with their painted angel bosses. "The night is still young!" he cried drunkenly, reeling about. His Fool's Cap was now slipping over one eye. Its tiny bells rang merrily. "And you must still obey me. I am still your rightful Lord!"

"Lord of the Pisspot!" someone bellowed from a dark corner. "Go stick your head down the privy—might sober you up!"

Filbert thrust his nose high in the air and put his hands on his hips. "I am the Lord of Misrule and by custom, I must be obeyed. And I have an idea of a game to play. As in that old crackpot storyteller's play—let there be a game of Hide and Go Seek! Everyone must play, even my Lord and Lady Lovell—and his esteemed guests, their Graces of Gloucester."

Francis started to sputter in the wine goblet a page has just refilled. Was the boy mad? Well, yes, crazed with drink, that was obvious to behold. "Don't be ridic…" he began, but Nan was tugging at his sleeve.

"You cannot gainsay him, Francis. What would people think? He may be a silly boy but he *is* the crowned Lord of Misrule. It's tradition!"

"But Nan, Christ's Nails, I hardly want people running around the house prying where they shouldn't…and…and destroying things. What if someone *did* get lost…"

Nan laid a finger on his lips. "Oh Francis, you worry too much about such things. It is only a game."

"It was only a game in that old varlet's ramblings too. And look at how the tale ended!"

"But that part is not real. None of us would be foolish enough to lock ourselves in a musty old chest!"

"No, but I could see someone drunkenly stumbling outside and freezing to death or falling in the Windrush and ending up drowned in the weir."

"As I said…you worry too much, husband. It will not happen." She reached out to gently squeeze his fingers. He was completely against this foolishness and beginning to long for the comforts of his bed but he would not deny her the joy of Twelfth Night. He knew how fleeting joy could be.

In the background, the revellers were clustering around the Lord of Misrule who was still shouting about Hide and Go Seek. Unfortunately, most of them, deep in their cups, looked quite eager. Glumly Francis walked over to the Duke of Gloucester. "Richard?"

Nan was swiftly at Anne's shoulder. "Cousin Anne, you want to play, don't you?"

"Why...why not?" said Anne. "I seldom have chance for such girlish fancies anymore!" She rose in her velvet gown with its patternings of golden pineapples, the long curtain of her veil falling over one shoulder.

Francis looked at Richard helplessly. "It is still Christmas," said the Duke. "Let them play. It is a time for joy. But not too late...we must all be up for Mass on the morrow and I dare say I am still saddle-sore from our long, cold ride from London."

Anne and Nan squealed like young girls, full of impish merriment, and took each other's hands. Standing together, the cousins looked very much alike, both ringed by the candlelight with their high clear brows and blue almond-shaped eyes. "You must both turn around and count to ten...no, make that twenty, our skirts are long," ordered Anne. "Then you must come and find us."

"It is not very dignified," said Richard. "Everyone will stare, hoping that I...I will trip on my shoes. You know how folk are—the greatest mirth of all would be to see a royal prince land on his arse." He pointed toward his feet; he was wearing very long Crakows with silver-capped tips.

"Oh *please*." Anne gave him a pleading look, which surprised him. He could not resist any more than Francis had resisted Nan earlier in the evening. He knew Anne was missing their little son Edward, back in Middleham; she worried too much over that boy, their only son. He understood; their lack of more children pained him too, especially when he saw Elizabeth Woodville producing a child almost every year for the King. He wanted to see her free of worry and in good cheer.

"Go, Anne," he said. "The Lord of Misrule decrees that you be merry—and your lord husband decrees it too."

Anne and Nan scurried from the Great Hall, surrounded by the rest of the riotous party and Filbert the Lord of Misrule. Up above in the minstrels' gallery, the musicians played a jaunty march. The Mummers, left to their own devices with only the servants and the glowering steward to chide them, remained in the chamber, picking through the uneaten and half-eaten food upon the tables, crunching on fish-tails and gnawing pork bones.

Francis beckoned the steward over. "Let that lot eat, Peter, it will make the voiders lighter at the end of the night! But make sure they don't run off with the family plate."

Then he turned back to Richard. "Let us go seek our wives and finish this Twelfth Night madness once and for all!"

The celebrants ran through the halls. Torches were doused to give them darkness to hide in. Giggles and laughter filled the air, and it was clear many young ladies were happy to be swiftly caught by the handsome young man of her choice.

Nan nudged Anne with her elbow. "Come, cousin, let's away from this crowd. Let me show you where we might hide."

Hastily she led Anne to a spiral staircase that ran up to the next floor. The torch bracketed over the first stair was out, leaving a sooty smudge on the wall; the spiral was lightless and silent. No one else from the party seemed to have passed that way.

"Make haste before anyone sees us!" Nan tugged on Anne's arm.

Skirts rustling, the two women mounted the stairs and ascended into darkness. A few minutes later, they were on the next floor near the apartments and the chapel. In the far distance, at the opposite end of the long corridor, they could hear voices raised in mirth and the sound of noisy footfall.

"This way," hissed Nan, pulling Anne back into the gloom. "We mustn't stay here—we'll be found in a trice. I know somewhere that is better than any other for hiding. No one goes there. I have only looked at it once myself when I first moved here with Francis."

She dragged Anne toward yet another staircase, narrower and darker than the one they had climbed earlier. Anne peered ahead into the gloom. "Are you sure we should?"

"Of course I'm sure! I do not want the men to find us right away. How dull that would be! I used to play games such as this with my sisters all the time—didn't you with Isabel?"

"Isabel," said Anne sadly. "No, seldom. She did not like 'running about' as she called it."

Nan remembered Isabel's yearmind had just gone by and gave her cousin a swift hug. "I should not have spoken of her. Forgive me, Anne."

The passed on to an upper floor. The ceiling sloped dramatically and it was darker than ever. "What is up here?" asked Anne, wonderingly. She coughed a little. The air was dry, heavy with dust.

"Nothing," said Nan, "but there's a room above, at the very apex of the house. You must see it. I have only ever viewed it once myself. Francis doesn't like to come up here. The dust...you see how thick and cloying it is."

She went to the end of the room, where a tiny wooden stair thrust up through a hatch. She climbed, the stairs creaking and pushed at the hatch with both hands. It was heavy, stiff.

"Perhaps we shouldn't," said Anne.

"I have seen it done," said Nan, and with a great effort, she pushed the hatch door open and climbed through, breathing heavily from her exertions but strangely triumphant.

Anne followed her, a little reluctantly, and once they were both in the attic chamber, Nan lowered the hatch door into its original position with a soft but heavy thump.

In this penultimate little chamber, perched at the top of the great house, lay hundreds of strange items—a fire-blackened beam with a carved angel half-eaten by wood-lice, a broken stone shield green with moss, the crumpled frame of a dilapidated bed, a screen painted with religious figures that had mouldered with age and dampness until the saints were nothing more than peeling blots. Faint blue light filled the cramped space from the narrow slash of a single small window set high up in the wall.

"I think all of this has been saved from the old Minster Lovell Hall," said Nan. "I do not know why; it would have been stored here by Francis' grandfather, William."

She walked across the floor; floorboards creaked, almost sounding like a groan. Anne jumped slightly and suppressed a nervous giggle. "Look, what's over here, Anne. There are chests, very old, wooden. I wonder what's in them." She dragged up a great fringed cloth made of a pale-yellow fabric—the bulk of it disintegrated at her touch, falling like gold dust to the floor to reveal a line of old oak boxes, sturdy and bound with iron that had turned blackish with age.

"I am not sure if I want to know," said Anne, thinking of the storyteller, Jack Rhymer, and his tale of the Mistletoe Bride who had died on her wedding night trapped in such a box.

"It is probably just more old fabric, like this coverlet." Nan flung the crumbling remains of the yellow fabric to the ground where it pooled like faded gold at her feet. "But it might be interesting. There might even be some salvageable cloth that we could take to our dressmakers."

"It's too dark to look," said Anne quickly. "We should come back tomorrow—bring candles or have a servant carry a torch. But we'd have to be wary of fire…"

"I do not think Francis would agree. As I said, it is not his favourite place."

"I am not sure it is mine either," said Anne, covering her mouth with her hand as she gave another cough.

Nan was examining one of the chests. It was long, low, almost coffin-shaped. "If that tale we heard tonight was true, the bride must have crawled into a casket such as this. Look how heavy the lid is…" She slid her fingers under the rim and gave a little tug.

"D-don't open it!" said Anne fearfully.

"Why not?" said Nan, with impish humour. "You surely don't think the mistletoe bride is still lying within, mouldering in her wedding dress."

"Ugh, Nan, when did you get such a morbid imagination…"

Suddenly there was a sound away in the gloom. A faint but insistent tapping, scraping noise. Faint scratching sounds, almost like fingernails, somewhere towards the rear of the room where the shadows lay thickest. Both women leapt back in alarm. The sound stopped as quickly as it had come.

Then Nan laughed, although rather shakily. "Mice, this part of the house is full of mice. Or...it's ivy...ivy tapping the wall. We've noticed some ivy growing on the building...Frances said a lad must be sent up to tear it off when spring comes as it harms the stone."

"Yes, yes, I am sure that's what it must be," said Anne. "Ivy...or a mouse. Nan, let's go. No one will ever find us here."

"That's the idea of the game, is it not?"

"Well...not quite. I assume that if the seekers are unsuccessful after a time, the hiders can emerge at the last and say they've won. Not that it matters....*it's just a foolish child's pastime.* I want to go find my husband, not crawl around in the dark like...like a rat..."

Again, there came the scraping, rattling noise, louder now, this time definitely drifting from the direction of the large chests flung haphazardly in the back of the attic room.

Both women now sprang towards the hatch that led to the lower floor. Nan knelt in the darkness, feeling around the edges of the oak panel. "Help me, Anne."

Clumsily Anne tried to get down beside her, impeded by the folds of her expensive gown. "What is it? What's wrong?"

"Nothing! I just cannot find the gap where I can raise the hatch. It was simpler to push it open from below."

Anne began to scrabble in the darkness. "We need a light. A light!"

"We haven't one. Here...here...Help me, I've found a loop of rope threaded through..."

The two women began to tug frantically on the rope, seeking to raise the heavy hatch door. Neither was used to such strenuous work; the knotted twine bit into their palms, chaffing and blistering. And then, suddenly, as they heaved, panting, the old worn rope snapped in two, sending them both tumbling backwards onto the dusty floorboards.

"Jesu! Are you harmed, Anne?" Nan scrambled around, trying to right herself.

"I …I think so…oh, I've lost my headdress…but I care nothing for that. I just want to get out of here!"

"Anne, hush for a minute. Listen!"

Anne fell silent. Far, far below, in the heart of the manor house, they could hear the sound of babbling voices, laughter, the squealing of pipes and horns. "They are still searching and they are coming this way!"

"Can they hear us up here?"

"I do not know. The room below us is empty too, as you saw…but we must try to summon them!" Frantically she began to pound on the floor with her hands, shouting between cracks in the boards and Anne joined her in earnest.

Both women began to feel flustered and light-headed with their continued efforts. Once cold in that unlit, fireless space, now a hot sweat of fear ran from them, making their breathing ragged, their brows fevered. As they pounded on the floor, dust flew up in clouds, reaching into nostrils and eyes, making tears stream and causing harsh, ragged coughing.

And behind them came the *scratch…scratch…scratch* of whatever was in the room with them. Louder than before, they thought, desperate—as if some creature long locked in the dark thought to escape that dusty tomb.

Panicked, they pounded harder, crying out to attract attention— but also to block the unknown noise coming from the shadows behind them…

Francis Lord Lovell was now in no happy mood. His house was full of revellers who had seemed to have lost all sense of propriety and his wife was missing. To say nothing of the Duchess of Gloucester. He glanced over at Richard, whose face was expressionless; the Duke said nothing but Francis, through long experience, knew that he was equally unnerved, holding back his true thoughts whilst his mind whirred on ahead. He was twisting the ring on his finger as he often did when agitated.

"I think my entire household has gone mad," Francis said in an apologetic tone. "There will be an end to it, Richard, I promise."

He pulled on a drapery that covered an embrasure in the hallway; behind it, a man and a maiden were kissing under the mistletoe. Both shrieked in alarm, the man's voice nigh as high as the girl's when they were discovered—and by the Lord of the Manor, no less. "Off with you," said Francis in the sternest tone he could muster. "This game is done."

Passing onwards, Francis and Richard discovered Filbert, the Lord of Misrule, collapsed against a wall, murmuring incoherently. Francis shouted for the rest of the squires to attend; they filled the corridor, grubby, sweaty and tipsy themselves. "Take him away—to the stables if you please. Dunk his head into a horse trough, if you must—that should wake him from his drunken stupor. Then put him to bed and make sure he stays there." He whipped the Fool's cap from Filbert's head and tossed it down the hall. "The Lord of Misrule is uncrowned. Morning will soon be upon us."

The two noblemen continued through the halls of the Minster. The noise of revelry was dying away now as the crowd dispersed. Some of the highborn were staying for the rest of the night; they retreated to their allotted chambers; the lower-born headed for the kitchens, where they could curl up near the still-warm overs, or for the stables. The patter of boots sounded on the icy cobbles outside, punctuated by roars of mirth when someone slipped.

"I think our wives have taken the storytellers' tale a little too much to heart," murmured Richard. His voice was calm but he was playing with his ring even more furiously. "Have you any idea, Francis? This is most unlike Anne."

"They are in the house somewhere. Where else could they be? They would not have been foolish enough to wander outside…" Francis halted, hating himself for allowing that uncomfortable thought in his head. Two women, partaken of wine, vanishing out into the snowy night. Hiding behind the frozen river-reeds, perhaps even deciding, in a fit of Twelfth Night madness, to skate upon the ice. The ice that would not hold a body's weight without cracking…

He noted Richard's shoulders, slightly uneven beneath his fine black doublet, stiffen. "We will keep searching, Richard. Mayhap they have merely lost track of the time. Talking…you know how womenfolk like to talk, and they are kin and have not seen each other for some time."

"Where else might we look? The chapel is empty and the apartments are now full of occupants. We have searched the kitchens, bakehouse and solar earlier on. We've looked in every nook and cranny, or at least it feels so—although you doubtless know the house far better than I."

"There is one more place," said Francis, looking thoughtful. "I have no idea why Nan would take Anne there, although I must admit…it *would make a perfect hiding place…*"

Nan and Anne were still banging on the jammed trap-door when Francis and Richard arrived on the upper levels of Minster Lovell Hall. They both fell back as they heard their husbands calling out to them and a moment later, the hatch banged open sending vast clouds of dust mushrooming into the air.

Gasping, they both hurled themselves down the narrow wooden staircase, almost falling over each other in their haste. Confounded, their husbands stared at them.

"Well…I guess you won the Hide and Go Seek game," said Richard dryly. "But Anne—your hair. What has happened to your headdress?"

"It was like in the story…the story of the Mistletoe Bride," gasped Anne. "We became trapped in the upper chamber with no way of getting out. We could scarcely breathe, no one seemed able to hear our cries and we could hear something scrabbling around in the darkness. It sounded as if it were trying to claw its way out of one of the old chests stored up there."

Francis glanced at Nan in astonishment, waiting for her confirmation. She nodded. "I thought the attic room would be a fine place to hide but I was wrong. And yes, we heard noises, both of us. I thought at first it was mice or the ivy outside but the sound kept coming. Getting louder and louder. And then we could not get out…"

"Shall I go upstairs and look?" said Francis, reaching for the dagger at his belt.

"No…no," said Nan, shaking her head. "Let's just leave things be and go back to the hall."

"Yes," said Richard, reaching out to put a steadying arm around Anne's shoulders. She already looked slightly embarrassed by her escapade; had she and Nan really been fearful of nought but the nightly noises of an old house in deepest winter? "The night is growing late, most of the company has departed to their lodgings. Tomorrow is Epiphany, a time of great joy for all Christendom. The only ghost any of us need worry about is...the Holy Ghost!"

Francis sputtered in surprise; it was most unlike his pious friend the Duke to make light of religion!

But his jesting comment broke the tenseness of the moment. Anne sniffed and toyed with her loose hair, falling nearly to her waist. "Forget my hat...I think it's been trampled on. As Richard said, Twelfth Night is over—we must look forward to Epiphany and less frivolity and foolishness."

"There will be Wassailers coming at noon tomorrow," said Nan brightly. "Singing in the orchard."

"I think I can deal with that," murmured Anne.

Lord Lovell, his wife and guests returned to the Great Hall, empty now save for servants clearing away the last of the debris. The Mummers, having availed themselves of all scraps worth taking, were filing in the direction of the door.

Their leader, Saint George, his face red and merry, began to sing as he strutted toward the cold night beyond the Hall,

"Now have good day, now have good day!
I am Christmas and now I go my way!
Here I have dwelt with more and less
From Hallowtide till Candlemas,
And now I must from you pass
Now have good day!
And to the good lord of this hall
I take my leave and of guests all,
Methinks I hear Lent doth call,
Now have good day!
Another year I trust I shall
Make merry in this happy hall,
If rest and peace in England fall
Now have good day...I am Christmas..."

And so Christmas' Twelfth Night passed and Epiphany beckoned, and Francis Lord Lovell, Richard Duke of Gloucester and their good ladies retired for a few hours before they rose again for morning Mass. Quietly they slept, undisturbed by any untoward thoughts, the excitement—and fear—of the previous evening behind them, a memory to be recounted with amusement on Epiphany Eves to come

But in the attic-room, the topmost pinnacle of Minster Lovell Hall, *something* scrabbled and clawed in the eternal darkness where the old wooden travelling chests were stored amidst detritus from the older building that had once stood on the site.

Scratch...scratch...scratch...

Surely it was only hungry mice. Or the wicked winter wind, streaming through cracks in the wall. Or the threads of tangled ivy tap-tapping as it sought entrance through the fabric of the house.

Or was it....

THE END

OTHER WORKS BY J.P. REEDMAN

MEDIEVAL BABES SERIES:

MY FAIR LADY: ELEANOR OF PROVENCE, HENRY III'S LOST QUEEN

MISTRESS OF THE MAZE: Rosamund Clifford, Mistress of Henry II

THE CAPTIVE PRINCESS: Eleanor of Brittany, sister of the murdered Arthur, a prisoner of King John.

THE WHITE ROSE RENT: The short life of Katherine, illegitimate daughter of Richard III

THE PRINCESS NUN. Mary of Woodstock, Daughter of Edward I, the nun who liked fun!

MY FATHER, MY ENEMY. Juliane, illegitimate daughter of Henry I, seeks to kill her father with a crossbow.

RICHARD III and THE WARS OF THE ROSES:

I, RICHARD PLANTAGENET I: TANTE LE DESIREE. Richard in his own first-person perspective, as Duke of Gloucester

I, RICHARD PLANTAGENET II: LOYAULTE ME LIE. Second part of Richard's story, told in 1st person. The mystery of the Princes, the tragedy of Bosworth

A MAN WHO WOULD BE KING. First person account of Henry Stafford, Duke of Buckingham suspect in the murder of the Princes

SACRED KING—Historical fantasy in which Richard III enters a fantastical afterlife and is 'returned to the world' in a Leicester carpark

WHITE ROSES, GOLDEN SUNNES. Collection of short stories about Richard III and his family.

SECRET MARRIAGES. Edward IV's romantic entanglements with Eleanor Talbot and Elizabeth Woodville

BLOOD OF ROSES. Edward IV defeats the Lancastrians at Mortimer's Cross and Towton.

RING OF WHITE ROSES. Two short stories featuring Richard III, including a time-travel tale about a lost traveller in the town of Bridport.

COMING SOON—AVOUS ME LIE. The childhood and youth of Richard III told from his first-person perspective.

ROBIN HOOD:

THE HOOD GAME: RISE OF THE GREENWOOD KING. Robyn wins the Hood in an ancient midwinter rite and goes to fight the Sheriff and Sir Guy.

THE HOOD GAME; SHADOW OF THE BRAZEN HEAD. The Sheriff hunts Robyn and the outlaws using an animated prophetic brass head. And there's a new girl in the forest…

STONEHENGE:

THE STONEHENGE SAGA. Huge epic of the Bronze Age. Ritual, war, love and death. A prehistoric GAME OF STONES.

OTHER:

MY NAME IS NOT MIDNIGHT. Dystopian fantasy about a young girl in an alternate world Canada striving against the evil Sestren.

A DANCE THROUGH TIME. Time travel romance. Isabella falls through a decayed stage into Victorian times.

THE IRISH IMMIGRANT GIRL. Based on a true story. Young Mary leaves Ireland to seek work…but things don't go as expected.

ENDELIENTA, KINSWOMAN OF KING ARTHUR. Life story of the mysterious Cornish Saint and her magical White Cow.

…And many other short stories and novelettes…

Printed in Great Britain
by Amazon

43203825R00026